For Brian Farran,
who cares about these matters, J.M.

For Nick, S.T.

Published in 2003 by Simply Read Books Inc.

Cataloguing in Publication Data

Marsden, John 1950-
  The Rabbits/John Marsden; Shaun Tan, illustrator
  ISBN 0-9688768-8-9
  I.Rabbits–Juvenile fiction.I.Tan, Shaun. 1974- II.Title.
PZ7.M368Ra j823 C2003-910261-0

First published by Thomas C. Lothian Pty. Ltd.

Designed by Shaun Tan
Cover design by Tony Gilevski
Colour reproduction by Chroma Graphics, Singapore
Printed in China by Leefung-Asco

THE RABBITS

John Marsden & Shaun Tan

Simply Read Books

THE RABBITS CAME
MANY GRANDPARENTS AGO

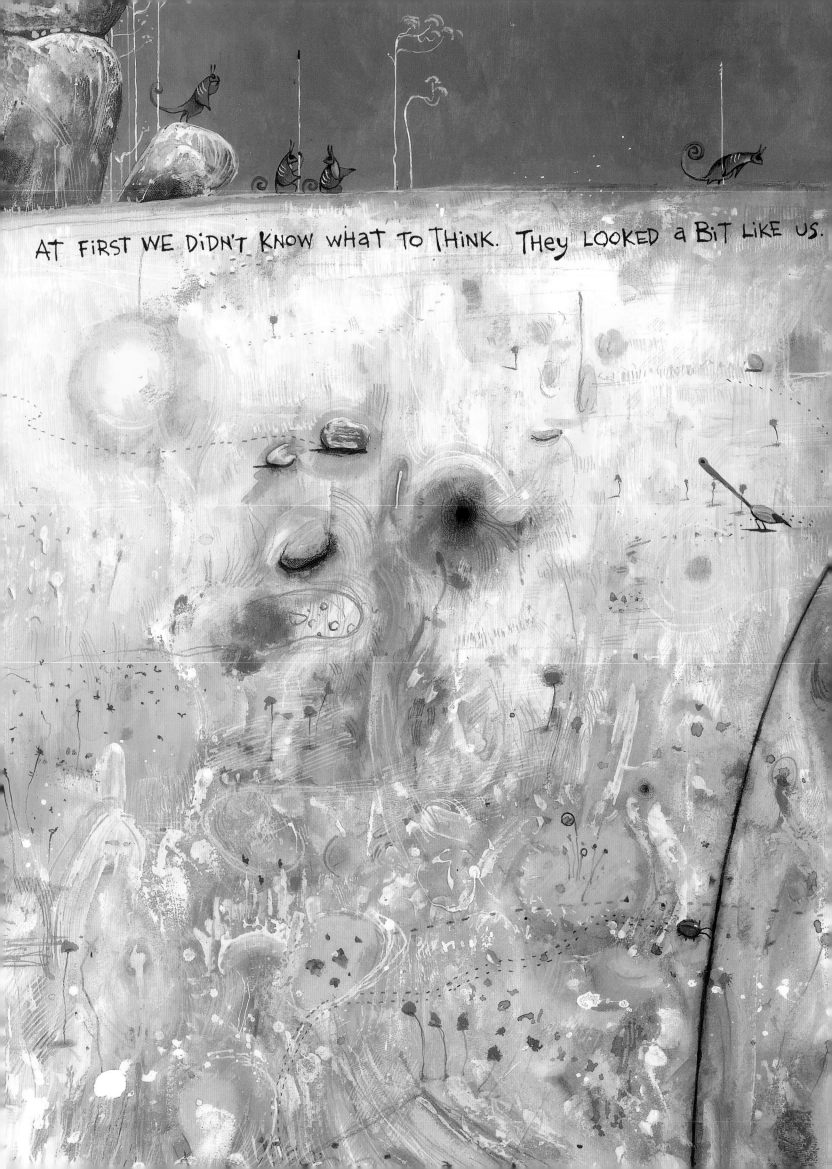

AT FIRST WE DiDN'T KNOW WHAT TO THINK. THEY LOOKED a BiT LIKE US.

THERE WEREN'T MANY OF THEM. SOME WERE FRIENDLY.

MORE Rabbits came...

THEY CAME BY WATER.

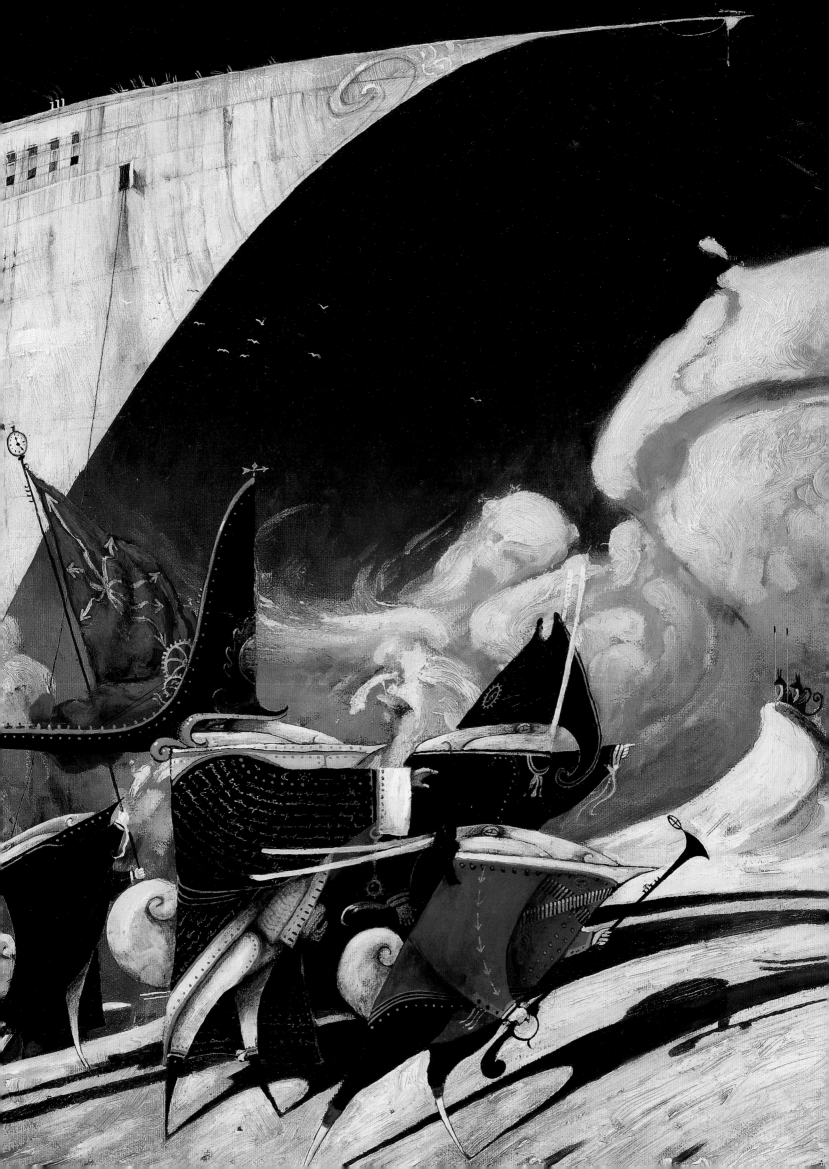

WE COULDN'T UNDERSTAND THE WAY THEY TALKED

WE LIKED SOME OF THE FOOD AND WE LIKED SOME OF THE ANIMALS.

BUT SOME OF THE FOOD

MADE US SICK

AND SOME OF THE ANIMALS SCARED US.

The Rabbits spread across the country.

NO MOUNTAIN COULD STOP THEM; NO DESERT, NO RIVER.

STILL MORE OF THEM CAME.

SOMETIMES WE HAD FIGHTS,

BUT THERE WERE TOO MANY RABBITS.

THEY ATE OUR grass.

THEY CHOPPED DOWN OUR TREES AND SCARED AWAY OUR FRIENDS.

RABBITS, RABBITS, RABBITS.
MILLIONS AND MILLIONS OF RABBITS.
EVERYWHERE WE LOOK THERE ARE RABBITS.

The Land is BARE and BROWN and The WIND BLOWS EMPTY across The PLAINS.

WHERE ARE THE LAKES,
ALIVE WITH LONG-LEGGED BIRDS?

WHO WILL SAVE US FROM THE RABBITS?